The Secret Home

by ANDY MIA KRANZ

For

Józef & Eleonora

Zygmunt, Franciszka & Henryk

Not so long ago
in a land far from here
lived a man by the name of Zygmunt.

As a boy,
he walked seven miles over the mountains to school
and seven miles back home —
even in winter when snow lay white and deep on the ground.

As a man,
he met, loved, and then wed a woman,
Franciszka.
Together they were blessed with a beautiful, bright child
and they named him Henryk.

Zygmunt, Franciszka and Henryk lived in a small village among the mountains
surrounded by forests of tall fragrant pines.

So begins this tale.

In this land
a war began,
bringing great upheaval.

Some men were forced into camps to work,
living in tents
behind fences.

Zygmunt was sent to a camp near his village
where men worked digging up pipes from old waterways
to re-use for the purpose of war.

Before he left
Zygmunt built a hiding place for Franciszka and Henryk,
carefully concealed behind a chest of drawers.
If danger came knocking
they could hide.

One day
Józef, a farmer,
returning from the village
met labourers working a few miles from their camp.

He told them of foreign soldiers
arriving in the village
rounding up their people
taking them away in crowded trains.

'Come up to my home in the mountains for the day,'
he invited.
'the soldiers won't look for you there.'

Zygmunt was one of the men.
He and Józef spoke that day.
Of the war.
Of their work.
Of the mountains they shared as their home.
The farmer asked of his family
and Zygmunt told of his beloved Franciszka
and their sweet young son.

Józef paused,
then said quietly
'This war is bad for your people.
Bring your family,
and my wife, Eleonora, and I will hide you here on our farm.
You are no longer safe in the village.'

So every Friday evening for three weeks
Zygmunt stole through the fence surrounding the camp
and walked up the dark hills,
where stars winked at him above the forest,
to the farm.

He and Józef worked and worked
all weekend.
Sweating,
digging in the heavy dirt,
making a hiding place.

They began in the cellar
set in a steep hillside behind the farm house.

They dug through the back wall of the cellar,
making a short tunnel
that opened into a tiny underground room.

Upon finishing,
they hid the opening of the tunnel
with a shelf full of jars, boxes, tools.

In the dark one night
the small family walked up to the farm,
winding through the silent trees, who witnessed their ascent.
Zygmunt carrying Henryk,
Franciszka carrying one small bag of clothes, books, treasures.

They entered the hiding place
to sit
to wait
to only whisper
to dwell by candlelight
to read, to tell stories, to draw, to play, to sing softly
to be quiet, to be patient, to pray for safety, to hope for peace.

Every evening after nightfall
the farmer and his wife came into the cellar
and tapped on the timber wall —
knock knock knock
knock
knock knock —
a sign all was safe.

Józef and Eleonora moved the shelf
and Zygmunt, Franciszka and Henryk crawled out from their hiding place.

They stretched their limbs,
washed,
and they ate their daily meal.

As the war pressed on, the village market closed.
There was just enough food growing on the farm
to share one meal each day,
a bowl of steaming potatoes.

After finishing their meal
they stepped quickly outside,
breathing in the cool air,
their eyes resting on the dark forms of the nightscape.
Seeing stars, shapes of clouds, mountains.
Seeing the moon.

The hiding place was too small for standing in,
with just enough room for them to sit.
And this is how they slept.
Close, embracing,
warming each other.

A long, thin pipe leading up to the meadow above
allowed in the cool, clear air.

On one cold night
Henryk was hot with a fever.
Wrapping him in a woollen blanket,
Józef hurried him in to the house
and lay him in a soft bed
under a trapdoor.

In the morning,
as Eleonora was spooning out warm soup for him,
the boy saw through the open trapdoor
a door
leading to the garden
left ajar.

He saw a stretch of green grass
bright in the sunshine!
And there,
a yellow flower
like the sun itself.

After being in the dark hiding place so long
he felt as if he was looking at a magical land ...

Henryk's health returned
and he went back into the small cave
where they spoke in whispers —
for they knew of soldiers always looking for people in hiding.

Once,
soldiers arrived.

Loud, sharp voices came from the cellar.
And other sounds —
boots scuffing the floor,
fists hammering the walls.

Zygmunt, Franciszka and Henryk were quiet and still.
Breathing hardly a breath.
Feeling their own hearts racing.
Sensing, in the quiet, each heartbeat.

But the soldiers did not chance to find the door to the secret home ...

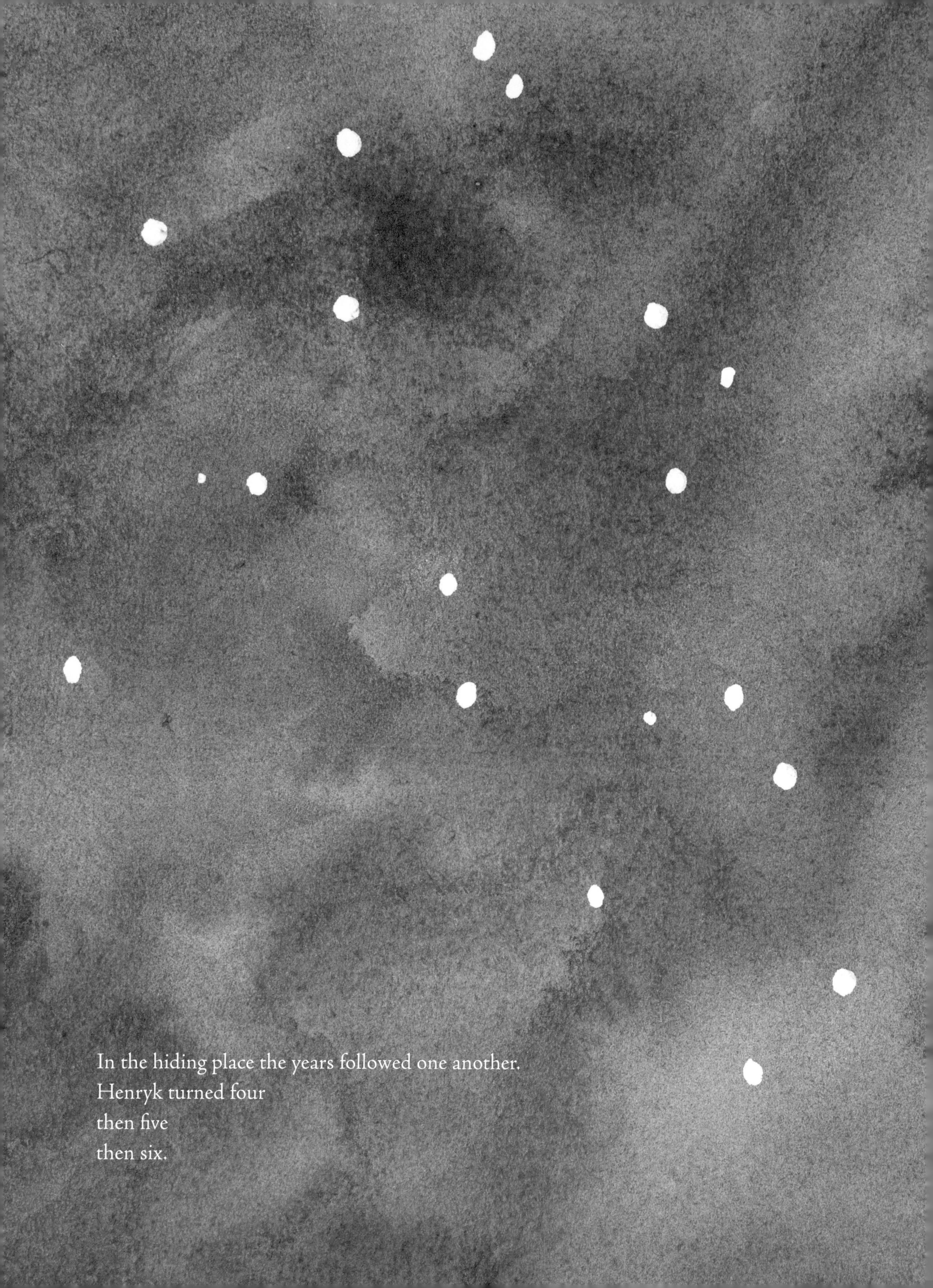

In the hiding place the years followed one another.
Henryk turned four
then five
then six.

When the family stepped outside one night
after their evening meal
they felt the earth they stood upon
shake with a sudden, thunderous sound.

Bombs!

Quickly they fell to the ground,
Zygmunt laying his body over his son's.
Face down on the earth, seeking its protection,
they heard the drone of planes
the whistling of falling bombs
the massive explosions.

Henryk could see bright flares of light,
hear the deafening noise
and feel the earth moving
from under his father's sheltering body.

Morning news on the radio declared:
The War has Ended!

Józef and Eleonora were sitting in their kitchen,
heard the radio,
bolted upright
and then ran

shouting
laughing
tripping

into the cellar
dragging aside the laden shelf
dropping jars
banging on the secret door
yelling that the war is over
crying tears of relief and joy!

This fine day
Zygmunt, Franciszka and Henryk
crawled out from their hiding place for the last time,
stood themselves up straight in the cellar,
walked out into the morning,
their eyes reeling in the brilliance of the light,
and were free.

They returned to the village.

They found their home gone
and all their loved ones disappeared.
Lost in the sadness that is war …

Weeping,
Zygmunt, Franciszka and Henryk retraced the path to the farm.

Embracing Józef and Eleonora
and their children,
thanking them for their
great kindness,
tears of farewell and sadness falling,
their journey began.

Through the pine trees and the mountains they walked,
a guide showing them a safe passage
unmarked by paths or roads
to cross the border unseen.

They passed farms, forests, towns, cities.

At the end of many roads
they found welcome at a camp.
A temporary home, full of people just like them —
lost and grieving
beginning again.

From here Zygmunt, Franciszka and Henryk travelled to a new home.
They cycled along fjords, found work, made new friends.
But when the rumblings of war sounded in a neighboring land
their fears awakened.

They arranged passage to yet another land.
This time
far,
far
away.

The three boarded a cargo ship,
sailing across many oceans,
breathing the sea air,
disembarking on to a long wooden pier on the other side of the world,
where they could live their lives
in peace.

Their skin felt the gold sunshine.
They listened to the birds' song
and the moving winds.

Their hearts healed
and flourished,
filled with the life they shared with their loved ones —
children, grandchildren, great-grandchildren.
An always expanding life as the generations unfolded
like the petals of that yellow flower,
an ever opening flower.

Zygmunt and Franciszka never forgot the kind farmers who had helped them.
They sent letters and gifts every year
until the day came
that Józef and Eleonora had both passed away.

Then they sent letters and gifts every year to their children
until the day came
that Zygmunt and Franciszka had both passed away.

And yet Józef & Eleonora
abide,
in the lives of their family
in the lives of the family they sheltered

and just here
as you and I
retell
this tale.

Dear J&E,
Thank you
...
Dziękuję
...
Józef &
Eleonora

The End

Afterword

/

This tale is true.

My father is Henryk.

Maybe because of his years in hiding he loves light, wide open skies and to be in the fresh air.

Our grandfather Zygmunt (we called him Zigushu) told us this story many times over while we sat on stools at his kitchen bench — he dipping bread into his coffee, we small girls listening, eating hazelnut wafers, entranced in the ritual he performed while he spoke of the time in hiding.

Franciszka was our Granny. She was small, imbued with wisdom; her eyes sparkled and her smile was wide.

//

The names of the farmer and his wife, Józef and Eleonora, sit on a mountain inscribed in the light-coloured stone of Jerusalem, alongside thousands of names of thousands of people who were just like them in courage and humanity.

///

Henryk returned to the land of his birth for the first time since he left as a boy, at the age of seventy-four.

He enquired and found the daughter of Józef and Eleonora living there.

They meet in a town not far from the farm — two people in their wisdom years.

They shared the small gems of what they recalled as children whose lives interwove in a time of war.

/V

Józef & Eleonora were named Righteous Among the Nations by Yad Vashem in 1994.

Thank you

Józef & Eleonora and children Aurleia & Wradyseaw, for your vast courage and kindness,
and for the all that you risked.

Sparke Helmore and lawyers Hannah Rose, & Georgia Murphy-Haste for Pro Bono legal assistance in establishing the not-for-profit company Secret Cave Projects, Ltd.,

Justice Connect for facilitating Pro Bono legal assistance,

Marin Accountants, Bernard Marin, Arthur Topalidis and James Oorloff for Pro Bono accounting advice and support,

Jayne Josem and the Jewish Holocaust Centre for sharing the images of survival in hiding,

The Arts Law Centre of Australia, Writers Victoria and the Australian Society of Authors for advice about the publishing process,

Myfanwy Jones, Jaye Kranz, Brooke Clark, Virginia Lowe, Abigail Nathan & Tegan Morrison for your careful and thoughtful editing at various stages of the manuscript development,

Chrisotpher Sanders for photographing the painitngs so beautifully,

And Kate vandeStadt for your lovely and creative design.

Myfanwy Jones for nurturing and following this book's journey so attentively,
Myfanwy again and Michaela Stubbs for your role as directors of Secret Cave Projects Ltd.,

Peter Long for wise advice on the way,

Ali & family for your generous support and friendship,

And the many dear friends who read the manuscript for this book and gave their encouragement.

Granny & Zigushu for evoking and retelling this story with such vividness, and for the years of love, care and joy,

My other grandparents Nana & Papa, Hanka and Naphtali, who also told us their stories of survival in hiding,

— together making up our personal history where human kindness and courage allowed for small miracles.

Dad for sharing your memories of these tender years of yours, and for supporting so gently this journey of your story to story book,

Both Mum and Dad, Emma and Henryk, for your enduring and deep wellspring of love,

Sidra Kranz Moshinsky and Jaye Kranz for sharing the kitchen bench at Clee Street, and for being there as all journeys unfold,

And to Iliya Kranz & Zev Kolker —

for revealing yet more depth to this story and my life since your beginnings,
and mostly, for your delight and your becoming.

Secret Cave Projects, Ltd. is a small Not-for-profit company set up specifically to govern the publishing, sale, translation and any other processes directly related to this book.

In the spirit of this story 10% of the cover price from the sale of each copy is donated to Not-for-profit organsiations providing humanitarian support to refugees and people seeking asylum.

For more information on this company and its governance visit thesecrethome.org.

First published in 2019 by Secret Cave Projects

Contact secretcaveprojects.org or andymiakranz@gmail.com.

Cover and text design by vandeStadt design

Editing by Myfanwy Jones, Jaye Kranz, Brooke Clark,
Virginia Lowe, Abigail Nathan & Tegan Morrison.

Illustrations photographed by Christopher Sanders Photography.

Printed and bound in China by 1010 Printing on
FSC certified 100% acid-free paper and printed with soy inks.

Typeset in Adobe Jenson Pro and Run Wild.

ISBN 978-0-6484985-0-6

A CIP catalogue number for this book is available from
the National Library of Australia

Published by Secret Cave Projects Ltd.
Melbourne, Australia

thesecrethome.org